That Alpaca Ate My Cracker!

Jane Riordan
Craig Shuttlewood

bookoli

It was **peaceful** in the mountains,

it was **peaceful** on the hill.

All was **calm**

and **quiet**

until ...

It's **YACCA THE ALPACA,** that's who!

With his head held **high** and slightly knocked knees.

His long white wool **BLOWS** in the **breeze.**

Yacca's fluffy tummy is **LOUD** and **rumbly.** He always seems to be **extremely HUNGRY!**

As **Yacca wanders off** in search of a **snack,**

He sees **BEAR** slurping **honey,** lying on his **back.**

Yacca **bounds** forward

and makes a daring

DASH ...

But **Yacca the Alpaca** simply goes on his way.

For **Yacca the Alpaca** it is a **HUNGRY** day.

A little while later, **Yacca** spies **another TREAT.**

It's **Armadillo,**

with juicy

FRUIT to eat.

With a

loud lip-smacking

SLIP,

SLOP,

SLAP...

Yacca **LEANS RIGHT** <u>in</u> and **steals**

the snack!

"That hungry **brute** **stole** my fruit!"

But **Yacca the Alpaca** simply goes on his way.

For **Yacca the Alpaca** it is a **HUNGRY** day.

Monkey is then spotted by **YACCA.**

He's quietly nibbling on a tasty **cracker.**

With a **GOBBLE,** **MUNCH**

and a

rather

GREEDY

crunch ...

But **Yacca the Alpaca** simply goes on his way.

For **Yacca the Alpaca** it is a **HUNGRY** day.

"I DO declare this has GOT to end, Yacca the Alpaca is not a kind friend."

The friends make a **plan** to set off and
CHASE.

"That **naughty** alpaca!"

So begins

the

GREAT

RACE ...

They follow a trail of crumbs that leads to the **Alpaca**.

But **Yacca** hears them coming,

and sets off with the cracker.

Monkey starts to chase,

Bear lumbers after.

(Armadillo wishes she was much faster.)

As they race along, they don't notice the

hump.

One by one they go

BUMP! BUMP ...

... THUMP!

The fruit is **squashed,**

the cracker is

crumbled,

The honey is

dripping,

everything is **jumbled.**

As they tuck in,

the new friends declare,

"Everything tastes

SO

MUCH

better

when you

SHARE!"